DINOSAUR Land

Lost in the Wild!

M.J.MISRA

For Seb Duxbury

EGMONT

We bring stories to life

Dinosaur Land: Lost in the Wild!
First published in Great Britain 2012
by Egmont UK Limited
239 Kensington High Street
London W8 6SA

ISBN 978 1 4052 6172 2

1 3 5 7 9 10 8 6 4 2

www.egmont.co.uk

A CIP catalogue record for this title is available from the British Library

Printed and bound in Great Britain by CPI

51207/1

EGMONT LUCKY COIN

Our story began over a century ago, when seventeen-year-old Egmont Harald Petersen found a coin in the street.

He was on his way to buy a flyswatter, a small hand-operated printing machine that he then set up in his tiny apartment.

The coin brought him such good luck that today Egmont has offices in over 30 countries around the world. And that lucky coin is still kept at the company's head offices in Denmark.

CONTENTS

An Amazing Secret!

Max Jordan flicked through the pages of his favourite dinosaur book as he sat in the waiting room of his parents' vet surgery. When he reached the picture of the edmontonia dinosaur, he frowned. The artist hadn't got the drawing quite right. Here, the dinosaur's body was a rusty brown, but edmontonias were greeny brown.

Max knew because he had actually met

six real edmontonias!

Max smiled, thinking about his amazing

secret. He had a magic fossil that could

whisk him away to a place called Dinosaur

Land, full of real, living dinosaurs! On his

first visit there he had met a girl called Fern

and her dad, Adam, who took care of sick

and unhappy dinosaurs. Max had been able

to help Adam and Fern with some of their

dinosaur problems, like finding a new foster mother for a baby allosaurus and helping a bactrosaurus with toothache. And he and Fern had become the best of friends.

Oh, I hope the magic fossil takes me back to Dinosaur Land soon, Max thought longingly. He really wanted some more dinosaur adventures!

Just then Max's dad walked into the waiting room with a lady and her puppy. The puppy scampered towards Max and started jumping up at him.

'Oh, goodness!' the lady gasped. 'Get down, Bramble. Behave!'

'It's OK,' Max smiled. 'I don't mind.'

'Bramble can be so naughty,' said the lady. 'He's so excitable and he is *always* chewing things up.'

'Try to keep him busy,' advised Max's dad. 'You can get special balls at the pet shop that you fill with dry food. As Bramble rolls the ball around the food will fall out.

It will take him longer to eat and stop him getting bored.'

The puppy wagged his tail.

'I think he likes that idea!' said Max with a grin.

'I'll go to the pet shop first thing in the morning,' said the lady. 'Thank you!' She paid her bill and left.

'Time for our supper,' Mr Jordan said, taking off his green vet's coat. He looked at Max. 'OK. Dinosaur joke time. How do you ask a dinosaur if it wants something to eat?'

'Easy,' Max said. 'Tea, Rex?'

His dad chuckled. 'Right, of course! Are there any dinosaur jokes you *don't* know, Max?'

'Nope!' Max declared. 'Hey, I've got one for you! What do you get when you cross a dinosaur and some fireworks?'

'What?' asked his dad.

'Dino-mite, of course!'

Back at their house, Max went up to his bedroom. His floor was covered with plastic dinosaurs. He had made a swamp out of old, green paper towels placed on plates filled with water, and trees from rolled up newspapers, painted green and brown. He had also used some cardboard boxes for barns. He'd tried to make it look as much like the real Dinosaur Land as possible.

Max started to set up a battle, with a stegosaurus and an einiosaurus facing a

T-Rex. He had never seen a real T-Rex, or any of the big meat-eaters in Dinosaur Land. Maybe he would get to meet one on his next trip!

'Let the battle begin!' Max said, charging the T-Rex and the stegosaurus together with a crash.

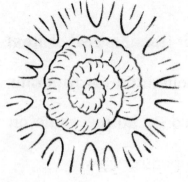

Then he picked up the einiosaurus.

Suddenly a light shone from on top of Max's bedside table. Max stared. The magic fossil was glowing. It could only mean one thing!

He jumped to his feet. The air buzzed and a silvery light swirled around him. Max shoved the einiosaurus into his pocket then ran to the table and picked up the snail-shaped fossil. His fingers started to tingle as he touched the grey stone. Excitement fizzed through him.

The magic was happening again!

Dinosaur Fun!

Bright sparks came whooshing out of the centre of the fossil and surrounded Max in a colourful cloud. He felt himself being lifted up and then he was somersaulting through the air as if he was on a fairground ride.

At last, his feet landed with a bump. Max blinked as the sparkling cloud cleared.

He opened his eyes wide. The sky above was bright blue and the sun was beating down. Far in the distance he could see a smoking volcano and a shimmering lake, and a forest of thick trees stood behind him. Max saw the path leading to Adam and Fern's stone

cottage, and the dinosaur sanctuary with its

wooden enclosures, barns and ponds.

'Oh, wow!' Max breathed. 'I'm in Dinosaur

Land again!'

He ran down the winding path and as he

passed between the white stones that marked

the sanctuary's entrance, he saw Fern. She was in an enclosure, sitting on the back of Trixie, the einiosaurus Max had met on his last visit. Trixie was the size of a rhinoceros, with greeny-grey skin, a leathery frill and two horns at the top of her head. She looked a bit like a triceratops but her third horn, on the end of her nose, curved down towards the ground instead of up. She was wearing a rope bridle and Fern was directing her with the reins.

Max ran over to the enclosure. 'Hey,
Fern!' he cried.

Fern's face lit up. 'Max! Hi!' she called
back. Fern had brown curly hair and
she was wearing trousers and a tunic made

out of pale skins. She leaned down and spoke to Trixie, and the dinosaur lumbered over to Max.

Max climbed over the fence. Trixie stopped in front of him and made a friendly rumbling noise in her throat. She greeted Max by touching him very gently with her nose-horn.

'Hello, Trixie,' said Max, stroking her rough cheek. 'Do you remember me?' Trixie blinked her small dark eyes and snorted.

'I think that's a yes!' Fern grinned. 'It's brilliant to see you again, Max. Down, Trixie!' she told the dinosaur. Trixie knelt on her front legs and Fern slid down the dinosaur's shoulder to the ground. She hugged Max. 'When did you arrive?'

'Just now. So, what's been going on here?' Max asked eagerly.

'Well, we've had quite a few new dinosaurs in the sanctuary,' replied Fern. 'There's a pterodactyl with an injured wing in one of the barns and an ankylosaurus called Basil with a damaged tail. We've released Wilfie, who you met last time. Oh, yes, and my little cousin, Joseph, is staying for a few days. I've told him all about you. He's five and he's really nice but he can be a tiny bit annoying. He never stops asking questions about the dinosaurs and he follows me around all the time. He'll be back in a minute. He's just gone to fetch Trixie some honey grass.'

Max nodded. 'He sounds like a lot of fun. So why hasn't your dad released Trixie back into the wild?'

Fern smiled. 'He tried, but she just kept coming back here! In the end Dad said she could stay. I've been riding her lots and now she lets me lead her too. Watch this!'

Fern used the bridle to lead Trixie round the enclosure. Even though Fern's head only came up to the top of the dinosaur's trunk-like legs, Trixie followed her obediently.

Max grinned. 'She's much better behaved than the puppy I just met at home.'

'What's a puppy?' asked Fern looking puzzled.

Max always forgot that Fern and Adam hadn't heard of most of the animals from his own world.

'It's a kind of baby animal,' he explained. 'They're little and bouncy. Hey, can I try leading Trixie?'

'Of course! Here!' Fern stopped Trixie and handed Max the reins.

'Walk on, Trixie!' Max said, tugging the reins gently. The einiosaurus didn't move. 'Come on!' he said, pulling again. But Trixie stayed absolutely still.

'Hmmm. Be careful,' said Fern. 'She sometimes does this and then she trots off suddenly and –'

The dinosaur charged forwards.

'Whoa!' Max cried as he was yanked off his feet. He clung on to the end of the reins, trying to keep up. 'Trixie! Stop!' His feet

skidded along the ground but the dinosaur

kept lurching forwards.

Max stumbled, fell on to the grass and let

go of the reins.

Trixie ground to a halt and turned to look at him in surprise. She snorted as if to say, *What are you doing down there, Max?*

Fern ran over giggling. 'Sorry! She's really good most of the time but then sometimes she just takes off like that. I think she likes pulling things around and once she goes there's no stopping her. She's so strong!'

Max got to his feet and patted Trixie. 'Next time I'll bring a skateboard and I'll be able to go as fast as her!'

'What's a skateboard?' asked Fern.

'It's a board that you stand on, with wheels underneath it.' Max saw Fern's confusion and grinned. 'Don't worry. It's hard to explain!'

Just then there was a shout. 'Fern!'

They looked round. A boy came running towards them, his arms full of greenery. He had brown hair and brown eyes like Fern.

'I've got some more honey grass!' the boy called to Fern. He reached them and stared at Max. 'Are you Max?' he asked.

Max nodded.

'Max, this is my cousin Joseph,' Fern said.

'I've been really wanting to meet you, Max,' said Joseph. 'Fern says you know lots about dinosaurs.'

Max didn't want to show off. 'Well,

I know a little bit.'

'He knows *loads*,' Fern told Joseph. 'Dad thinks the fossil Max owns brings him here so he can help us with any dinosaur problems we have.'

'Wow! Like magic!' Joseph breathed.

'Hey, I wonder why I'm here this time?' said Max. 'Are you having any trouble?'

Fern grinned. 'Why don't you come and meet the new dinosaurs and see?'

Basil the Ankylosaurus

'Come on. Let's go and look round,' Fern said to Max.

'But Fern!' Joseph said. 'You told me that if I got the honey grass I could have a ride on Trixie.'

'Maybe later,' said Fern.

'But I've never ridden a dinosaur before

and you promised!'

'Not now, Joseph,' Fern replied. 'Taking Max round is more important.' She took the honey grass and put it on the ground. Trixie put her head down to eat and Fern slipped the bridle off. 'Come on, Max!' she said.

Joseph ran after them. 'So, why does Trixie have a frill on her neck?' he asked.

'I don't know.' Fern shrugged. 'She just does.'

'I think it's for protection,' Max explained,

remembering his dinosaur fact book. 'In case another dinosaur attacks her.'

'So why doesn't she have spikes on her back like some dinosaurs?' Joseph asked curiously.

'Because different types of dinosaur have different ways of defending themselves,' Max replied.

'And why is she green? And why does she have a horn that goes downwards and why –'

'Joseph!' Fern groaned. 'Stop asking Max

so many questions!'

'But I really want to know the answers!' said Joseph.

They were interrupted by a loud bellowing noise.

'What's that?' asked Max.

'It's Basil the ankylosaurus,' Fern replied, pointing to a nearby enclosure. Standing near the fence was a dinosaur about as tall as a man, staring out towards the forest in the distance. He had a very small head with two little horns sticking out at the sides, a short neck and a wide body covered in spiky plates. His thick tail had a row of spikes along it too, and it was round at the end, like a club. His tail had a bandage on it. Basil lifted his head and bellowed sadly again.

'Why is he making that noise, Fern?' asked Joseph.

'Because he wants to be back in the wild,' she replied. 'But we can't set him free until

his tail is healed. He's really bored.'

'Can we go and see him?' Joseph asked eagerly.

Fern smiled and nodded. 'Yes, I think he'd like that.' Joseph gave a little cheer of delight and ran on ahead.

Basil bellowed again.

Fern sighed to Max. 'Maybe that's why you're here, Max. Basil is certainly becoming a problem. He's so unhappy.'

Max knew all about ankylosauruses. 'You can't set him free yet because he needs his clubbed tail to fight off predators, right?'

Fern nodded. 'Ankylosauruses swing their tails around and that big bit at the end crashes into the legs of attacking dinosaurs.

If Basil can't use his tail he won't be able to protect himself and it could be really dangerous for him. Dad thinks we may be able to release him next week but we'll just have to see. We're worried he's going to try and break out of his pen before then.'

While they had been talking, Joseph had climbed into the pen. He ran over and patted Basil's leg. The dinosaur swung his head round to greet the little boy and his nose knocked him flying by mistake. But

Joseph just laughed, jumped to his feet and gave Basil another pat.

Max looked around the enclosure. 'Basil doesn't seem to have much food,' he said,

noticing that the grass was very short and all the lower branches of the trees were stripped of leaves. 'Maybe if he had more he might not be so bored. I'm sure I read that ankylosauruses are grazing dinosaurs. That means they like to eat all the time.'

'Well, this ankylosaurus is a very *greedy* dinosaur,' said Fern. 'He's already eaten everything in the enclosure. Dad's building him a new one at the moment. We've tried

putting extra food in for him but he just guzzles it all down really quickly.'

Basil started to pace up and down the fence, swinging his head from side to side.

'Oh dear,' Fern said, watching him. She raised her voice. 'Joseph, you'd better get out of the pen! Basil's not looking happy.'

'What's Basil doing?' Max asked.

'It looks like he's thinking about charging the fence,' Fern said anxiously as Joseph

scrambled out of the pen. 'We'd better go and tell my dad. We're going to have to do something about him, but I've no idea what.'

Max's brow was wrinkled in thought, but suddenly his eyes opened wide. 'I think I've got an idea!' he said.

Fern blinked. 'What is it? Tell me, Max!'

Max's Idea

Max was thinking back to Bramble the puppy and what his dad had said about putting the puppy's food in a ball to help keep him occupied. Perhaps they could do something like that for Basil. Max turned to Fern. 'Maybe we can stop Basil being bored by hiding his food in something, or making it into a game. What do you feed him on?'

'Leaves and long grasses,' Fern replied, looking puzzled.

Max thought fast. 'How about we hang the grass from a rope? We could tie it to the tree branches and it would bounce around as he tried to eat it. It'd be more fun for him and he'd eat a lot more slowly. It might stop him standing around and thinking about breaking free all the time.'

'It's a brilliant idea!' said Fern, looking excited. 'Let's go and ask Dad if we can try it. Joseph, come on! We need to go and see Dad. Max has had an idea that could help Basil.'

The three of them ran to find Adam.

Joseph couldn't run as fast as Max and Fern so they had to keep waiting for him.

'Come on!' Fern called. 'Hurry up!'

'I'm trying!' panted Joseph. 'Why do we have to go so fast?'

'We have to get to Dad quickly before Basil breaks out!'

'Hold our hands,' Max said. 'It'll be much quicker that way!'

Max and Fern held on to Joseph's hands and helped him run along with them.

They found Adam over by some trees. He was cutting some of them down to get wood for Basil's new enclosure. He was delighted when he saw Max with Fern and Joseph.

'Max, what a nice surprise! So the magic fossil has brought you here again!' he said. 'I wonder what you're going to help us with this time?'

'Max has already had an idea to help Basil,' said Fern. She and Max quickly explained the plan.

Adam looked pleased. 'Well, that certainly sounds worth trying! There's some rope in the barn, and some fresh ferns and grasses.'

'We'll get to it straight away!' promised Max.

'Can I help you?' Joseph asked.

'Of course you can, Joseph,' said Adam, ruffling Joseph's hair.

'But, Dad!' Fern protested. 'He slows us down and he's too little to help. Can't he stay here with you?'

Adam frowned.

'Please!' Fern begged. 'I haven't seen Max for ages and I want it to be just us for a little while. I've been looking after Joseph all day.'

'All right, all right. Just for now,' said Adam reluctantly. 'But you must let Joseph join in with you later.'

'Thanks, Dad!' Fern cried. 'We'll get back to Basil!'

Max couldn't help feeling guilty. Glancing back he saw that Joseph was looking upset.

'Couldn't we let him come with us?' he said as he hurried after Fern.

'But why? It'll be much more fun on our own,' said Fern. 'Don't worry about him. He likes helping Dad. Come on!'

Soon, Max was so busy that he forgot about Joseph. He and Fern fetched some rope and a pile of long, cut grass from the feed barn. When they got back to Basil's enclosure the dinosaur was facing the fence.

'At least he hasn't tried to break free yet,' said Fern.

They went into the enclosure. Basil stamped the ground with his front foot and lowered his head.

'What do we do now?' asked Fern.

'Let's use the rope to tie the grass into a big bundle,' said Max. 'Then I'll climb one of the trees and you can stand on the wheelbarrow and throw the end of the rope up to me. I'll tie it to the branches. If we tie three or four different bundles up he'll be kept pretty busy.'

They started to put the grass into bundles. Basil came to see what they were doing. His eyes lit up as he saw the food, and he grabbed a big mouthful.

'Hey, naughty!' said Fern, nudging him, but Basil just kept chomping away at the grass. In the end they had to put a pile of grass in one corner to keep him away while they worked. He munched through it happily.

Fern was right. He really was greedy!

When they had the bundles ready, Max climbed up a tree and Fern stood in the wheelbarrow. She threw the end of the rope over a thick branch and Max crawled to reach it. While Fern lifted the grass bundle, Max used all his strength to pull it high. Then he wrapped the rope round the branch and knotted it as firmly as he could.

'I'm glad Basil isn't a diplodocus!' Max puffed as he tied up the third bundle.

Diplodocus dinosaurs were really tall with long necks. 'I'd need to climb a very high tree then!'

'I've got a joke,' Fern said. 'What do you do if you see a blue diplodocus?'

'Cheer him up!' Max grinned. 'How can you tell if there's a diplodocus in your wardrobe?'

'I know that one!' said Fern. 'The door won't shut!' They both laughed.

'This is fun,' said Fern, her eyes shining.

Max climbed back down the tree. Basil had finished all the grass in the corner and had ambled over.

'What do you think, Basil?' Fern asked him.

Basil looked at the bundle of grass with interest and tried to take a mouthful. He caught a bit with his teeth but then the bundle swung out of reach. He followed it but it swung back before he could reach it. The dinosaur gave it a puzzled look, and chased after it again. He managed to grab some more with his teeth but it swung away and then back again, hitting him on the head. Basil looked surprised for a second but then he grabbed another mouthful.

'I think he likes it!' said Max.

'Fern! Max!' They heard Joseph's voice and looked round to see him and Adam at the fence.

'That seems to have worked well. Basil looks much happier now,' said Adam.

Max smiled. 'Thanks. That's one problem solved, I guess. Is there anything else I can help with?'

Adam stretched his muscles. 'I wish you could help me find a way to shift the logs! I'm aching all over from pulling the cart.'

'I helped you, Uncle Adam,' said Joseph.

Adam smiled. 'You did, Joseph.'

'I like being helpful,' Joseph declared.

Max thought for a minute. 'Maybe there is a way to make it easier. You need something to pull the cart for you . . .' His eyes widened. 'What about Trixie!' He turned to Fern. 'You said she loves learning new things. Couldn't you train her to pull the cart?'

'I could try!' Fern gasped.

'It would be great if she would. I'd be

able to build enclosures much more easily.
Why don't you two go and see if she'll do it?'
suggested Adam.

'And me?' asked Joseph eagerly.

'Yes, and you,' Adam agreed. 'I have to
go outside the sanctuary and check on the
herd of edmontonia, but I don't need Trixie.
I can walk there. You'll need to stay here
with Fern and Max though, Joseph. It will be
too far for you.'

'Oh, great,' Fern muttered to Max.

'I'll see you later,' Adam said and strode off.

'Can we go and try to train Trixie?' Joseph said excitedly.

'I think you'd better just watch, Joseph,' said Fern. 'Trixie sometimes takes off and you might get hurt if she charges around. But you can see from the fence.' She turned to Max. 'Let's get her bridle and some ropes.' They fetched everything they needed and went in to Trixie's enclosure. First, Fern put the bridle on the einiosaurus and then they attached extra ropes to the sides.

'I'll hold the ropes and see if she'll pull me. If she does that, we can try it with logs or a cart,' Max said.

He took hold of the ropes and pulled backwards while Fern encouraged Trixie to walk forwards.

'*Please* can I help?' Joseph called from the fence.

'No, we don't want you to get hurt,' said

Fern, concentrating on Trixie, who had stopped moving. 'Walk on, Trixie. Pull!'

'But I want to be helpful,' said Joseph.

'I'm sorry, Joseph, but can you go and do something else?' said Fern. 'Max and I really need to work on this.'

Joseph gave a big sigh and wandered off, dragging his feet in the dust.

Fern patted Trixie. 'Come on, Trixie, let's try again. When I say "pull" you've got to walk forwards. PULL!'

This time Trixie did take a step forwards,

dragging Max behind her.

'Oh, well done! Good girl!' Fern cried.

'Pull again, Trixie. Pull!'

Trixie soon got the hang of it. She was

ready for the next step, so Max tied the ropes

to a big, broken branch on the ground.

'Come on, girl,' Fern called to her. 'Pull it

towards me!' Sure enough, Trixie lumbered

forwards to Fern. The dinosaur gave a happy

snort, as if she knew she had done well.

Fern turned to Max, her eyes shining. 'Oh, wow! It's working! Soon she'll be pulling the cart, and that will make everything so much easier for Dad. This was a great idea!'

Max beamed and patted Trixie.

'She's probably done enough for now,' said Fern, undoing the ropes and taking off the bridle. 'Let's give her a rest.'

'We should go and find Joseph,' said Max.

'I bet he's gone to see Basil,' said Fern.

They headed to Basil's enclosure. But as they got closer, Fern gasped. 'Max! Look!'

They both stopped and stared. The gate was open and the dinosaur had gone!

Missing!

'Oh, no! Where *is* he?' Fern cried in alarm.

'He must have got out!' said Max. He ran to the gate. There were dinosaur footprints in the bare soil. They were leading in the direction of the sanctuary entrance. 'Look at these!'

'But how could he have got out? How

would he have opened the gate?' wondered Fern. Then she hit her head with her hand. 'Joseph! Of course! He must have let him out. But why would he do that? And where's he gone? Oh, Max, you don't think he's followed Basil, do you? What are we going to do? Basil can't defend himself at the moment, and if Joseph followed him anything could happen to him. A meat-eater could attack them out in the wild.'

'Quick, let's go after them!' Max started

to follow the dinosaur prints. Maybe they could reach Joseph and Basil before they got into serious danger.

As Max and Fern reached the two white stones at the entrance they saw Joseph running towards them from the forest. Max breathed a huge sigh of relief. At least Joseph was safe!

'Joseph!' exclaimed Fern. 'Are you OK?'

'I'm fine,' he gasped. 'But Basil's escaped. He's gone into the forest!'

'What happened?' demanded Max.

Tears filled Joseph's eyes. 'He'd finished the grass you hung up and he was looking bored again so I thought I'd take him for a walk, like you do with Trixie.'

'But, Joseph!' Fern exclaimed. 'I haven't trained Basil to lead. What happened next?'

'As soon as I opened the gate he ran off. I couldn't stop him. He galloped into the forest. I ran after him but he was too fast,' Joseph said.

'You went near the forest? But it's so dangerous out there!' Fern ran her hands through her hair and swung round to Max. 'Oh, Max. What are we going to do about Basil? He could be hurt . . . killed . . .'

'I'm really sorry, Fern. I was just trying to be helpful!' Joseph cried.

Fern turned on him. 'Helpful? You've ruined everything! Oh, I wish you'd never come to stay with us!'

Joseph sobbed and ran into the sanctuary.

'Joseph! Come back!'
Max shouted, setting off
after him.

'Leave him!' Fern grabbed Max's arm. 'It's Basil who needs us now. He's in the forest with no protection. He could be in real danger.'

Max realised she was right. They could go after Joseph later. But a thought struck him. 'Even if we do find Basil, how will we bring him back?'

'Sugar cane!' cried Fern. 'I know it's bad for dinosaurs' teeth but all the plant-eaters love it and he's bound to come with us if we have some. Let's go and get some from the house!'

Armed with handfuls of sugar cane, Fern and Max ran out of the sanctuary. Two paths led into the forest.

'Which one should we take?' said Fern.

Max looked at them carefully. The one to

the right was clear and wide but the path to the left was overgrown with trees, ferns and creepers, bushes and flowers. Which way would a hungry ankylosaurus go?

'Let's try this one!' he said, pointing down the overgrown path. They set off, and as they ran Max saw that some of the branches were broken, as if a dinosaur had recently walked past. Then he spotted a dinosaur footprint.

'I bet that's Basil's. This way!'

They hurried towards the tall trees.

The branches overhead blocked out the sun and creepers hung down all around them. The air was warm and damp and massive green ferns were growing everywhere.

'We'd better be careful,' said Fern, looking uneasily into the shadows. 'Meat-eaters live in these woods and we must watch out for sinking swamps. They look like solid ground but they're very deep and if you step into one the thick water sucks you down. Dad never lets me come here.'

Max swallowed but there was no way he was turning back. They had to find Basil! 'Come on!' he said bravely.

They walked on.

Suddenly they heard a trumpeting noise coming through the trees to the right. Max jumped.

'Don't worry, it's just a stegosaurus,' said Fern.

Max gave a sheepish grin and carried on. They turned another corner.

'Basil!' they cried together. The missing ankylosaurus was on the path right in front of them. His head was plunged deep into a patch of long grass. He looked up when he heard their voices, tufts of greenery hanging out of his mouth.

'Basil, you're OK!' said Fern in relief.

She ran to him and hugged his neck, being careful to avoid his spiky sides. Basil smelled the sugar cane in her pockets and started nuzzling her.

'That's right,' Fern told him quickly. 'Come with us and you can have some yummy sugar cane.' She pulled some out from her pocket and held it to him.

Basil took one step towards her, then another.

'Here's some more,' said Max. He handed Fern some from his pockets and, step-by-step, they lured the dinosaur back to the sanctuary. It took every bit of sugar cane but finally Basil was back in his enclosure.

Max shut the gate with a relieved sigh.

'Phew!' He felt exhausted.

Fern fed Basil the last of the sugar cane
and climbed over the gate. 'At least we got

him back safely. We'll have to give him some more bundles of food so he doesn't get bored again.'

'Yes, but first let's go quickly and find Joseph,' said Max. 'I bet he's still really upset. We can leave some leaves scattered on the ground to keep Basil busy for now.'

Fern looked a bit guilty. 'Oh, dear. I shouldn't have shouted at Joseph like I did. I was just so worried and cross. I wonder where he's gone?'

They started hunting around, calling Joseph's name, but there was no sign of him.

'Maybe he's in the house,' suggested Max.

They went to the cottage but it was quiet, cool and empty. 'Let's get a drink and then go and check the barns,' said Fern.

She fetched a jug of lemon juice and took it over to the table. As she poured the juice into two stone cups, Max noticed something on the table. It was a piece of grey slate with something written on it in chalk.

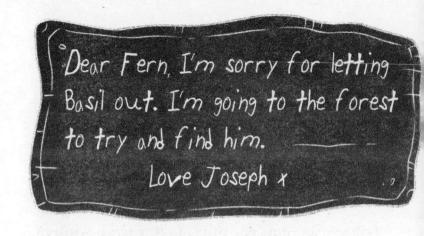

Dear Fern, I'm sorry for letting Basil out. I'm going to the forest to try and find him.
Love Joseph x

'Fern! Look!' Max showed her the slate.

Fern's face went pale. 'Joseph's in the forest? But it's so dangerous there!'

'We'd better go and get your dad,' said Max, running to the door.

'Wait, Max! We haven't got time,' said Fern. 'Dad's still out with the edmontonias and the longer Joseph is in the forest the more likely something is to happen to him. We've got to find him ourselves. Let's ride Trixie. She can go much faster than we can on foot.'

Max nodded, his heart beating fast. 'Good idea.'

'Oh, Max.' Fern had tears in her eyes. 'What if we don't find him?'

Max swallowed. He didn't want to think about that.

Trixie to the Rescue

Trixie looked surprised to see them. Fern slipped the bridle on to the dinosaur's back and asked her to kneel while she and Max mounted. Then she clicked her tongue. 'Walk on, Trixie,' she said.

Trixie's stride was long and lumbering and Max lurched from side to side.

'Faster!' said Fern.

Trixie broke into a run. Max almost slipped right off her back.

'Hang on tight!' yelled Fern.

'I'm trying!' muttered Max.

He grabbed Fern and hung on for all he was worth. It was like riding an elephant! Every step Trixie took made his body judder.

Fern steered Trixie towards the trees. 'Joseph must have used the other path or we'd have seen him when we were getting Basil back,' she said.

She turned Trixie down the wide, clear path. They had been racing along it for a few minutes when Trixie stopped dead. Max and Fern almost tumbled off.

'What are you doing, Trixie?' asked Fern.

Trixie lifted her head and snorted. Fern nudged her with her heels but the dinosaur wouldn't move.

'Trixie, come on!' Fern urged. 'Don't start being naughty now!'

'Maybe she's not being naughty,' said Max, feeling how tense the dinosaur's muscles were beneath him. 'Maybe she can hear something. There could be danger ahead.'

Trixie swung into the thick bushes at the

side. Fern pulled the reins but Trixie paid no attention. A tree branch banged into Fern. Max reached back to his friend just in time to stop her falling off.

'Careful, Trixie!' Fern cried.

But Trixie just went further into the bushes. The branches closed around them.

'What's she doing?' exclaimed Fern.

'Ssh, Fern!' Max hissed. Trixie was still staring at the track through the branches. She was normally so well-behaved. He was sure there must be a good reason for her to be acting so strangely.

'Let's keep quiet,' he whispered.

Trixie gave a soft snort as if she agreed with him.

Fern opened her mouth to speak but froze as a large dinosaur on two legs came stalking down the path they had been on a few moments before. Max felt his blood turn to ice. The dinosaur was a meat-eater. Its head was massive and its small eyes

were savage. It stopped and looked around, flaring its nostrils and swinging its head from side to side. It looked like a smaller version of a T-Rex. It opened its mouth and Max saw its large yellow teeth.

'That's a dryptosaurus,' breathed Max.

'They're really vicious.'

Fern nodded and Max saw her fingers trembling on Trixie's reins.

Max's heart thudded. If the dryptosaurus realised they were there, they wouldn't stand a chance.

Please go away, please! he begged silently.

The dryptosaurus looked round, almost as if it could sense them. It paused for a moment, but then moved on down the path, its head thrust out in front of it as it looked for prey.

Max didn't dare move but after a few minutes he felt Trixie relax.

'It's gone I think,' said Fern.

All the breath rushed out of Max.

'That was very close!'

'Too close!' Fern bit her lip. 'What about Joseph? Oh, I hope he's all right! What if that dryptosaurus or another meat-eater finds him?'

Trixie stepped cautiously out of the bushes and lumbered back on to the path. She set off in the opposite direction to the dryptosaurus. Max wanted to shout out Joseph's name, but what if that brought the dryptosaurus back?

Suddenly they heard a faint yell through the trees to the right. 'Help! Help!'

'Joseph!' exclaimed Max and Fern together.

Trixie headed into the trees towards Joseph's voice. She trampled bushes and ferns, and barged through thick curtains of creepers, until she came to a clearing and stopped.

There was a swamp in the clearing and Joseph was sinking into it. He was hanging on to a large branch but only his head and arms were above the thick, green, swampy water.

'Fern!' Joseph gasped.

'Joseph!' Fern shouted. 'Hang on! We'll get you out of there! Down, Trixie!'

The dinosaur knelt and Max and Fern scrambled off.

'Fern!' cried Joseph. 'I can't get out!'

Fern and Max ran to the edge of the swamp but Joseph was too far out for them

to reach. He looked terrified as he kicked

and struggled.

Fern looked at Max desperately. 'Oh, Max,

how can we get him out?'

But for once Max was out of ideas. 'I don't

know.' His eyes were wide with panic.

'Help me!' Joseph cried. 'Please. I'm going

to drown!'

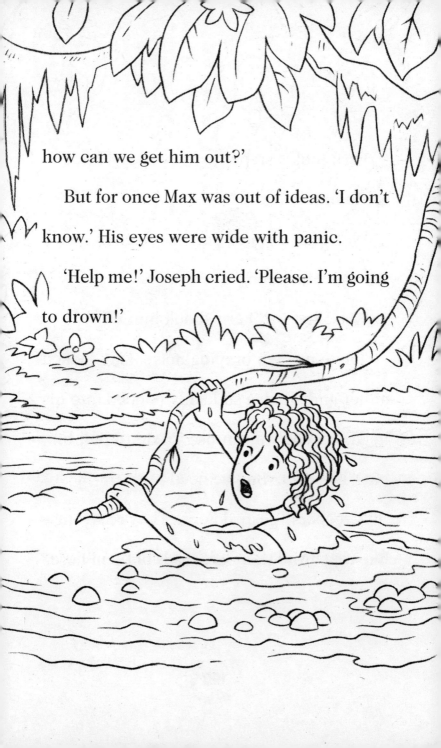

Fern took a step into the water. 'I *have* to get to him.'

'No!' Max stopped her. 'If you go in, you'll only get stuck too.'

'Max! Let go!' Fern shook him off.

Trixie made a braying noise. Max looked at her and an idea suddenly popped into his head. 'Maybe we can use Trixie to pull him out!' he cried. 'But we need rope.'

'Creepers!' gasped Fern. 'They're strong – like rope. And there are loads of them here.'

She ran to a nearby tree and started to climb up it. 'I'll cut some down.' Pulling a small knife from out of her pocket, she hacked through a bunch of creepers. They fell to the ground with a slithering sound. 'There you go!' said Fern.

Max grabbed them. There wasn't a moment to lose. 'Hang on, Joseph!'

'I can't hold on much longer!' the boy wailed.

Max swirled one of the creepers around

his head like a lasso and threw it towards the boy. His first throw fell short. Max pulled the smelly, wet creepers back and tried again. He threw even harder. This time they landed near Joseph.

'Grab hold, Joseph!' Max shouted.

Using all his strength, Joseph lunged for the end of the creeper and clung on.

Fern had reached the ground again and she attached the other ends of the creeper to Trixie's bridle.

'Pull, Trixie. PULL!' she cried.

Trixie snorted, then started to walk forwards.

'Hang on tight!' Max cried to Joseph. The creepers tightened with Joseph's weight and Trixie slowed down.

'Come on!' Fern encouraged the dinosaur. 'You can do it, girl!'

Trixie set her shoulders and pulled again. With each step she took, she tugged Joseph closer to the side of the swamp. Max knelt.

The swamp water smelled horrible but he

didn't care. He leaned out as far as he could

and as soon as Joseph was within reach, he

grabbed him. There was a massive squelch as Max pulled the younger boy out on to the dry land.

'We've done it!' Max yelled.

Fern came running over. 'Oh, Joseph!' she said, hugging him despite his wet and smelly clothes. 'I'm so glad you're OK!'

'You . . . you saved me!' gasped Joseph.

'I'm really sorry I shouted at you,' said Fern, still hugging him.

'Where's Basil? Is he OK? Did you find him?' Joseph asked anxiously.

'He's fine – he's back in his enclosure,' said Fern. 'We found him eating some grass.'

'How did you end up in the swamp?' asked Max.

'I was going along the path when I heard a roar. I could tell something was coming towards me and it sounded fierce, so I just jumped into the bushes and started running away. I wasn't looking where I was going and I ran straight into the swamp. The more I tried to get out, the more it sucked me down. Luckily the branch was there for me to hang on to.' Joseph looked really upset. 'I'm sorry, Fern. And Max,' he said, glancing at Max. 'I'm sorry you had to come and rescue me. I just wanted to try and get Basil back.'

Fern hugged him again. 'I know. I know

you were trying to help. I should never have told you to go away when we were training Trixie. You don't know enough about dinosaurs yet to be doing things on your own, but you will. I'll teach you, I promise, and then you'll be able to help lots.'

'Really?' said Joseph hopefully.

'Really,' answered Fern. 'Now, come on, how about we ride Trixie home.'

Joseph's eyes lit up. 'I can ride her?'

Fern smiled. 'You can.'

Home Again

Max, Fern and Joseph rode home together on Trixie's back. To Max's relief they didn't see the scary dryptosaurus again. After today, he knew he would much rather see meat-eaters from a distance!

As they rode through the gates, Adam came striding towards them. 'Where have you been?' he asked anxiously. 'I've been really worried about you. I came back from seeing the edmontonias to find that all of you had disappeared! Look at the state of you. You're soaked! What's been going on?'

'It's a long story,' said Max.

'It was all my fault,' said Joseph.

'No, it was mine,' said Fern. She quickly told her dad what had happened.

Adam's annoyance turned to relief as he heard the tale. 'It wasn't the cleverest thing you've ever done but thank goodness you're all OK. It was very brave of you both to go and try to rescue Basil and Joseph, and very lucky you'd been training Trixie to pull things. But Fern, you must learn to be more patient with Joseph.'

'I won't ever go off on my own again,' promised Joseph. 'And I won't try to take a dinosaur for a walk either!'

'I'm going to teach Joseph all about dinosaurs,' said Fern to her dad. 'Then he won't make mistakes any more.'

'Well, that sounds like an excellent plan,' said Adam. 'Now, let's go inside. You all look like you could do with something to eat and drink.'

They went into the cottage and Adam poured some fruit cordial and gave them some honey-seed biscuits.

'These are delicious!' said Max.

Adam smiled at him. 'I wish I could give you more to say thank you. First you helped to solve our problem with Basil, then you thought of an easier way to build enclosures, *then* you helped rescue Joseph from a swamp! You've been busy! I'm very glad the magic fossil brought you to see us today.'

'Me too!' said Max, thinking of everything that had happened. He'd ridden a dinosaur, trained a dinosaur and seen a fully grown meat-eater. It felt like he'd been there a week!

Max felt a tingling in his pocket. He put his hand in and pulled out the magic fossil, which was nestling next to his toy einiosaurus. Bright lights were sparking from the fossil's shell.

'I must be about to go home,' he said,

getting to his feet.

'I don't want you to go, Max!' cried Joseph. 'What if I'm not here next time you come? I might never see you again!'

'Here,' Max said, reaching into his pocket and pulling out the einiosaurus. 'You can keep this to remember me.'

'Thank you!' gasped Joseph. He turned it over in his hands. 'It's just like Trixie!'

'Oh, come back soon,' Fern said to Max. 'I'll miss you!'

'Say goodbye to Basil for me,' said Max. 'And think of some more jokes while I'm gone!'

A multi-coloured whirlwind whooshed around him. 'Bye!' he yelled as he was whisked away.

He felt himself bum he ground, and the cloud cleared. Max saw that he was back in his bedroom. He looked around. It was very strange to be here after all the excitement of Dinosaur Land! The model dinosaurs and their enclosures were still laid out and the stegosaurus and T-Rex were lying together on the floor where they had crashed into each other. Nothing had changed because no time passed in the human world when he was in Dinosaur Land.

'Max!' his dad's voice shouted up the stairs. 'Time for tea!'

'Coming!' Max shouted back. He looked back down at his model dinosaurs, then

at his magic fossil, and traced the ridged pattern on it with his fingers. 'Please take me back soon,' he whispered.

Slipping the fossil into his pocket, he smiled and ran downstairs.

EGMONT PRESS: ETHICAL PUBLISHING

Egmont Press is about turning writers into successful authors and children into passionate readers – producing books that enrich and entertain. As a responsible children's publisher, we go even further, considering the world in which our consumers are growing up.

Safety First
Naturally, all of our books meet legal safety requirements. But we go further than this; every book with play value is tested to the highest standards – if it fails, it's back to the drawing-board.

Made Fairly
We are working to ensure that the workers involved in our supply chain – the people that make our books – are treated with fairness and respect.

Responsible Forestry
We are committed to ensuring all our papers come from environmentally and socially responsible forest sources.

**For more information, please visit our website at
www.egmont.co.uk/ethical**

Egmont is passionate about helping to preserve the world's remaining ancient forests. We only use paper from legal and sustainable forest sources, so we know where every single tree comes from that goes into every paper that makes up every book.

This book is made from paper certified by the Forestry Stewardship Council (FSC®), an organisation dedicated to promoting responsible management of forest resources. For more information on the FSC, please visit **www.fsc.org**. To learn more about Egmont's sustainable paper policy, please visit **www.egmont.co.uk/ethical**.